Mrs. Goodstory

By Joy Cowley

Illustrated by
Erica Dornbusch

Boyds Mills Press

Text copyright © 2001 by Joy Cowley
Illustrations copyright © 2001 by Erica Dornbusch

Published by Caroline House
Boyds Mills Press, Inc.
A Highlights Company
815 Church Street
Honesdale, Pennsylvania 18431
Printed in China

U.S. Cataloging-in-Publication Data
   (Library of Congress Standards)

Cowley, Joy
    Mrs. Goodstory / by Joy Cowley ; illustrated by Erica
Dornbusch.—1st ed.
[32]p. : col. Ill. ;   cm.
Summary: A young boy explores the world through stories
with Mrs. Goodstory.
ISBN 1-56397-774-5
1. Stories—Fiction.   I. Dornbusch, Erica, ill. II. Title.
   [E] 21 2001   AC   CIP
00-103740

First edition, 2001
The text of this book is set in 16-point New Baskerville.

10 9 8 7 6 5 4 3 2 1

In memory of Dr. Kent Brown, Westfield, N.Y.,
who was very fond of a good story.
—J.C.

To Ken, Kaitlyn, Taylor and Karen
for their unquestioning faith and encouragement.
—E.D.

ON DAYS OF WONDER Mrs Goodstory travels with flowers in her hair. Her bag is full of knicks and knacks, and her skirts rustle like the pages of a thousand books.

"Come," she says, taking my hand.

I ask where we are going,
but she will not tell me.

"Stories should be full of surprises," she says.

We find a path through a forest where parrots
hang upside down arguing with one another in loud
squeaks and squawks. Mrs. Goodstory opens her bag
and throws out crumbs of language, which the birds
catch in clacking beaks.

    Mrs. Goodstory knows that parrots love words.

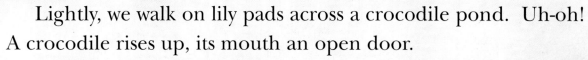

Lightly, we walk on lily pads across a crocodile pond. Uh-oh!
A crocodile rises up, its mouth an open door.

"Enough of that!" says Mrs. Goodstory,
tapping it on the nose.

Back it slurps into the water, bubbling rude words.

"Whoever wrote that crocodile should have given
it better manners," Mrs. Goodstory says.

Animals run past us, giraffes and golden-eyed
lions, zebras that flicker like picket fences in
moonlight. An elephant trumpets alarm, and
flamingos rise up from the river in a pink cloud.
     "Something has frightened them,"
I tell Mrs. Goodstory.

Thudding down the trail comes Dead-eye Dayton on his mustang. "Yee-haw!" he yells, waving his hat in the air.

Mrs. Goodstory tries to stop him. "Wrong story! Wrong story!" she cries, reaching into her bag for an eraser.

"I don't mind if you don't mind," I tell her. "You said stories should have surprises."

The flowers in her hair nod as she puts back her eraser, and Dead-eye Dayton rides on after the elephants and zebras and lions and giraffes.

On another wondrous day Mrs. Goodstory and I explore the sea, swimming with seals and diving with whales. We can breathe underwater, and we don't get cold or wet. That's the way it is with stories.

Captain Kent asks us if we would like a ride to the Arctic Ocean on his icebreaker.

"How far is it?" I ask.

"Only two pages," he says. "We'll skip the boring parts."

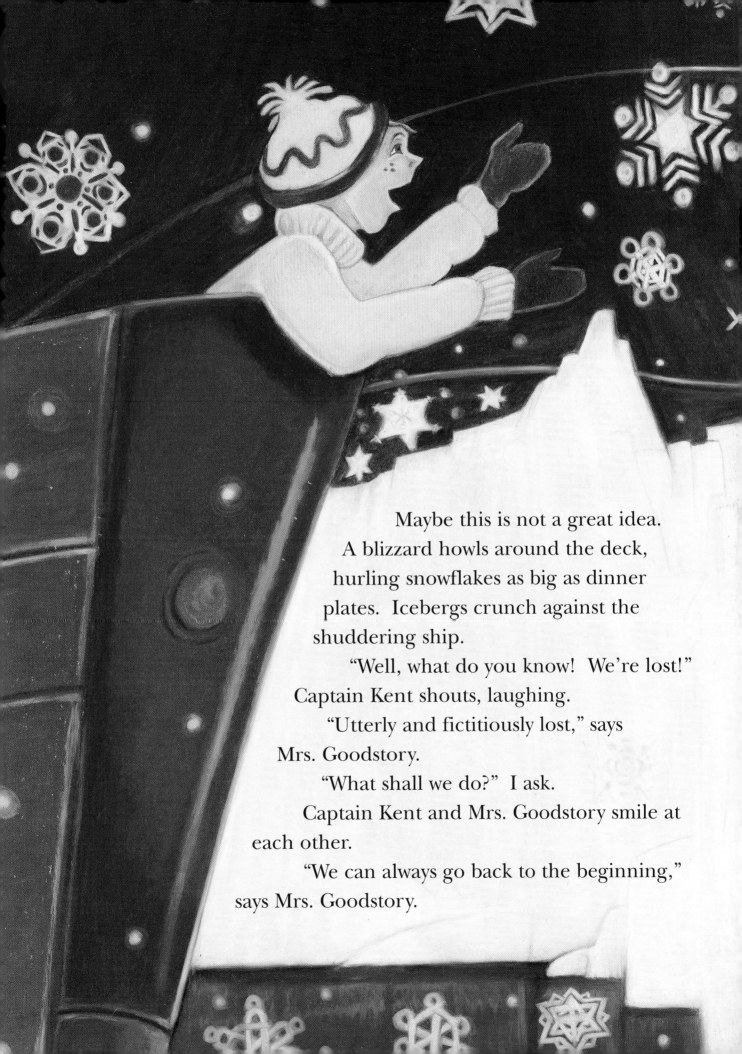

Maybe this is not a great idea.
A blizzard howls around the deck,
hurling snowflakes as big as dinner
plates. Icebergs crunch against the
shuddering ship.

"Well, what do you know! We're lost!"
Captain Kent shouts, laughing.

"Utterly and fictitiously lost," says
Mrs. Goodstory.

"What shall we do?" I ask.

Captain Kent and Mrs. Goodstory smile at
each other.

"We can always go back to the beginning,"
says Mrs. Goodstory.

As we wave good-bye to Captain Kent, Mrs. Goodstory says that stories only appear to be dangerous.

"A fine adventure never hurt anyone," she says.

"I know that," I tell her. "But I don't like being lost, not even in a story."

The next time, we get lost midair. True as frog spit. We are soaring high above the city, peeking into pigeons' nests, when Mrs. Goodstory says, "I can't remember what happens next."

We stop moving. Hand in hand, we hang above the street like a couple of parade balloons.

"Think! Think!" I beg.

She wants to rummage in her bag, but I will not let go of her hand.

"I knew it a speck ago," she says.

"Make up something!" I yell.

"You make up something," she says.

As fast as a blink, I make up an old biplane. The pilot is
my friend Patti, who will know how to fly through a tricky
story. Under the plane I hang a ladder like a swing, and
then I make up a circus tent where we can be the final act
in a trapeze show.

Patti brings us down to a cheering crowd.

"Bravo!" says Mrs. Goodstory.

"A perfect ending!"

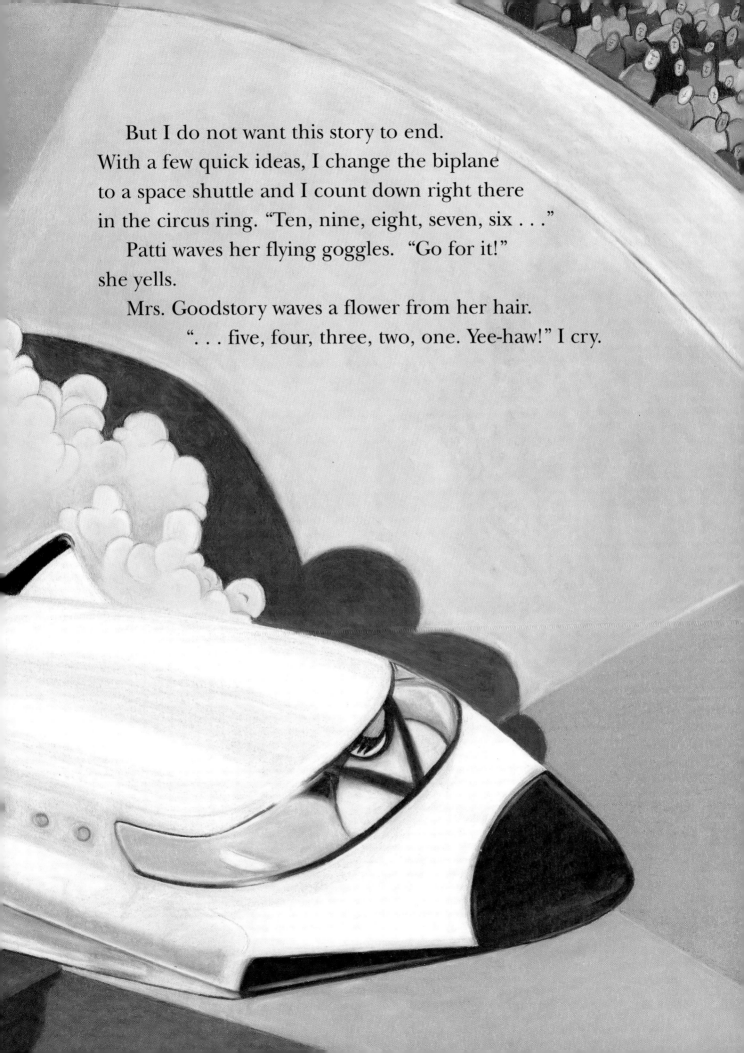

But I do not want this story to end.
With a few quick ideas, I change the biplane
to a space shuttle and I count down right there
in the circus ring. "Ten, nine, eight, seven, six . . ."

Patti waves her flying goggles. "Go for it!"
she yells.

Mrs. Goodstory waves a flower from her hair.

". . . five, four, three, two, one. Yee-haw!" I cry.

On my first solo story, I circle the moon twice.
I'm thinking about landing, when a cluster of
asteroids comes flying out of nowhere. CLUNK!
KAPOW! Red alert! I am out of control! My shuttle
is hit by a story surprise!

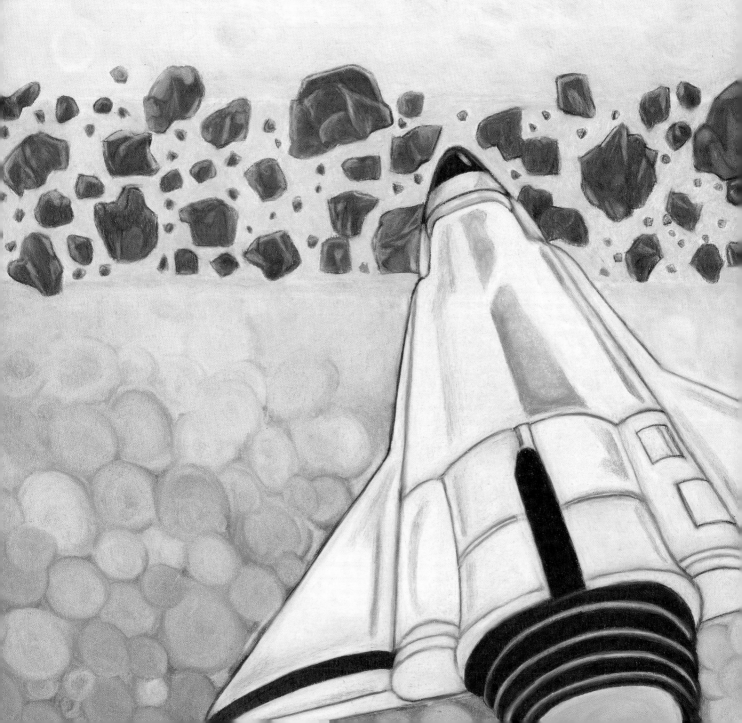

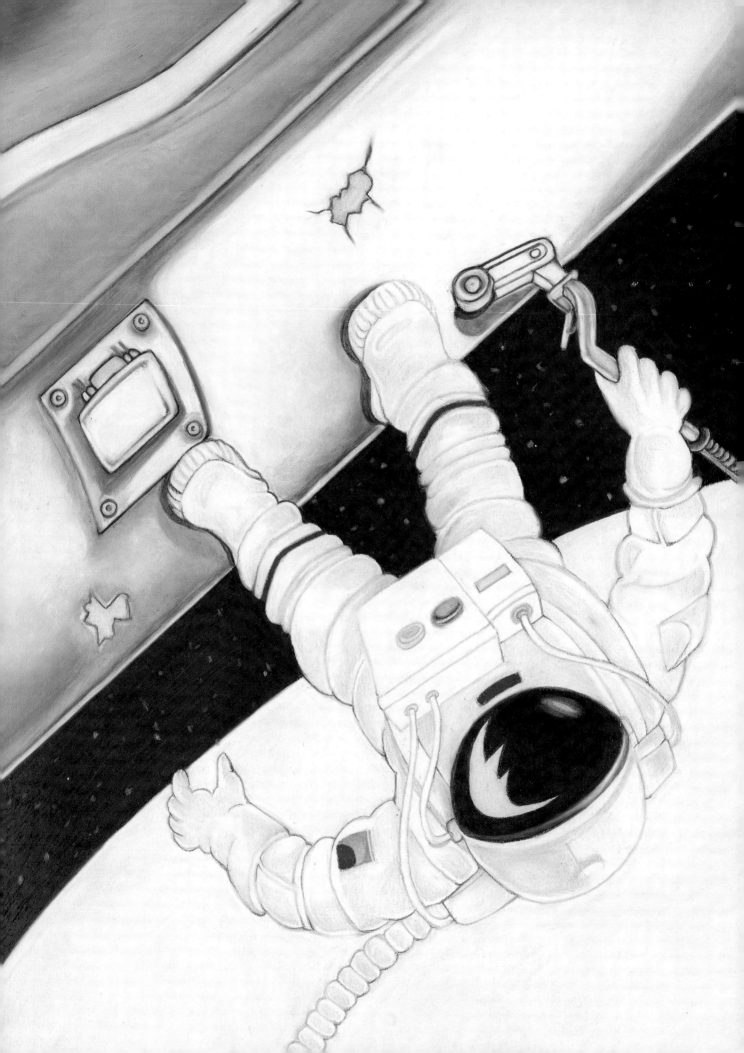

I see the trouble. Asteroids have hit the fuel
tank. I need to spacewalk to patch the holes. No
problem. It takes only a minute to make up the
tools and parts I need. My magnetic boots clunk on
the silver shuttle. The moon hangs under my head
like a big white dish. If I do these repairs quickly,
I can be back on Earth in time for lunch.

Mrs. Goodstory is in the kitchen making banana muffins. She understands why I had to land my space shuttle by her petunias.

"Stories often go their own way," she says, giving me the bowl to lick. "But don't you worry a speck about that. If you follow a good story, it will always bring you home."